THE JEWEL IN THE SKULL

THE JEWEL IN THE SKULL

Adapted by

James Cawthorn

from the story by

Michael Moorcock

Big O Publishing/Savoy/London

To my Father, James Cawthorn Snr.

First published in 1978 by **Savoy Books**
for **Big O Publishing Ltd.**
219 Eversleigh Road London SW11 5UY
Telephone 01-228 3392 Telex 914549

American distribution by **Big O Publishing**
Box 6186 Charlottesville VA 22906
Telephone 804-977 3035 Telex 822438

German distribution by **Big O Verlag GmbH**
Hohenzollernstrasse 122, 8 München 40
Telephone 089-303134 Telex 5216019

Savoy Books
18 Peter Street Manchester M2 5GR
Telephone 061-928 6929

ISBN 0 861300 06 8

Printed in England by Lowe & Brydone Printers Ltd

IN THE AGES THAT FOLLOWED

THE TRAGIC MILLENIUM

The landscapes of earth grew old and strange. Where once the great nations of Europe had ruled, a mosaic of minor kingdoms fought and flourished. Far beyond their borders lay vast, shadowy lands of mystery. And from the Isles of Granbretan came the first stirrings of a new power,

THE DARK EMPIRE.

Over them all brooded

THE RUNESTAFF,

the legendary artifact which controlled the patterns of human destiny. Where it resided, and from what lost era it came, no one knew. Yet to swear by the Runestaff was the most compelling oath which a man could lay upon himself. It was irrevocable . . .

CLAD IN DARK METAL, helmeted in beastmasks, the armies of Granbretan stormed the shores of Europe. Across the silver bridge spanning thirty miles of sea, product of their bizarre and sophisticated science, flowed a ceaseless river of men, horses and machines. Through the skies flapped swarms of ornithopters, pouring down red fire from slender flame-lances. At the head of the host rode the most feared Warlord of the Dark Empire, Grand Constable of the Order of the Wolf and First Chieftain of the armies under King-Emperor Huon —

BARON MELIADUS OF KROIDEN.

From a hill overlooking the ancient town of Aigues-Mortes, COUNT BRASS watched his people riding to the Summer Festival. Once the greatest warrior-statesman in Europe, he had retired to the wide, rich marshlands of the Kamarg, and at the wish of the inhabitants had become their Lord Guardian.
ONLY HE FULLY UNDERSTOOD the complex and powerful weapons which he had installed in the towers girdling the province. Against them, no European army could prevail. But the strength of the Dark Empire was an unknown quantity. Already they had ravaged the Northern Kingdoms and were spreading in a widening arc across the Continent. Secure in his fortified lands, however, Count Brass was untroubled by distant conflict.

Guardian flamingoes wheeled overhead, their riders saluting the Count.

He rode into Aigues-Mortes; up to the hill crowned by Castle Brass.

Frowning, he studied the strange carriage in the castle yard.
"Dark Empire workmanship . . . what brings their nobles to our small province?"

YISSELDA OF BRASS called to him:
"Father, we have visitors. Baron Meliadus of Granbretan and his men!"

BOWGENTLE, the philosopher-poet, the Count's friend and adviser, said: "So — the infection spreads to the Kamarg!"

"We will be courteous," said Count Brass. "We have no quarrel with the Emperor of Granbretan."

Baron Meliadus turned, removing his wolf-helm in acknowledgement of their rank.

"Forgive my unheralded intrusion, Count Brass. To Europe's greatest hero, I bear greetings from the immortal Huon, King-Emperor of Granbretan."

UNTIL THE ARRIVAL OF MELIADUS, Count Brass had looked upon Granbretan as the one force capable of realising his dream of a united Europe. He had chosen to see only a superb military machine, directed by ruthless strategists. Bowgentle, studying the patterns of history, saw instead a unique menace, a nation of brilliant madmen whose ultimate destiny was to impose the rule of chaos upon the entire planet.

Now, in conversation with the Baron, Count Brass became increasingly aware of disturbing qualities in the Granbretanian's nature . . .

Yisselda hurried to her third rendezvous with Meliadus.

A tremendous swing drove the blade from his grasp!

He waited calmly for the final stroke.

"Bowgentle!" cried Yisselda. The poet gasped: "My dagger-hilt checked the blow."

Baron Meliadus left Castle Brass that night. Knowing that he lived only by the mercy of Count Brass, he was possessed by a deep and malevolent rage.
"I will break Count Brass . . . as wife or slave, Yisselda will be mine . . . and I will make a furnace of the Kamarg! This I swear by the Runestaff!"

IN GILDED CHAINS, THE DUKE DORIAN HAWKMOON VON KÖLN MOVED UPRIVER between the gloomy Towers of Londra, capital city of Granbretan. Last survivor of the family which had ruled a fair German province, he had seen his parents butchered and the fertile lands laid waste by the soldiers of Baron Meliadus.

BY PRETENDING TO THROW IN HIS LOT WITH THE CONQUERORS, he had contrived to raise a rebellion. On the verge of victory, his forces were crushed by hastily-summoned ornithopters. Captured, he now faced the vengeance of the Lords of Granbretan. Yet he walked as in a trance, devoid of hope or fear . . .

At the quay, pig-masked gaolers waited.

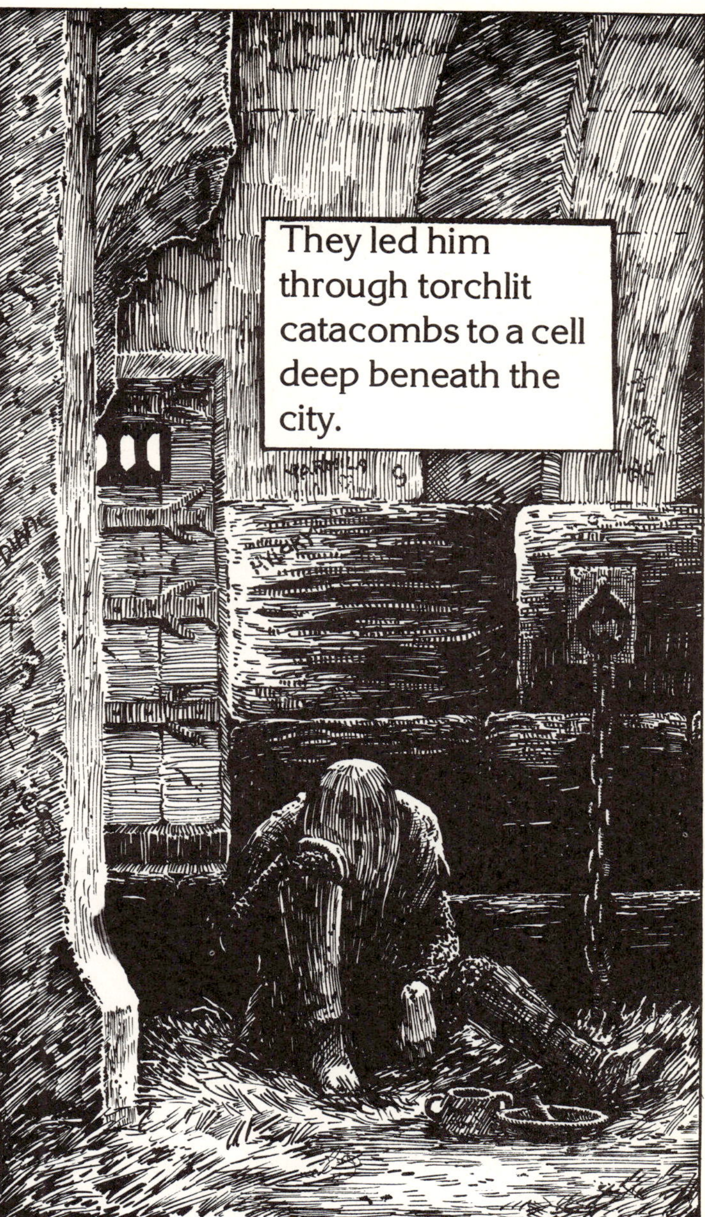
They led him through torchlit catacombs to a cell deep beneath the city.

BUT NOT FOR LONG. Baron Meliadus had found the weapon he needed to gain revenge upon Count Brass. A slave took his order to the Prison Master.

Some days later, Meliadus came to the quarters to which Hawkmoon had been transferred. "So, Duke von Köln — you are well again. Do you know me?"

"I am well," Hawkmoon said, vaguely. "But I do not know you."

Disconcerted, Meliadus snapped: "It was I, Baron Meliadus of Kroiden, who slew your father! It was I who burned your homeland of Köln!"

Goaded by Hawkmoon's strange apathy, Meliadus uncovered his face: "You live only by my command, Lord Duke! Is your spirit dead? Have you no anger?"

"You think, perhaps, that I have lost my reason?"

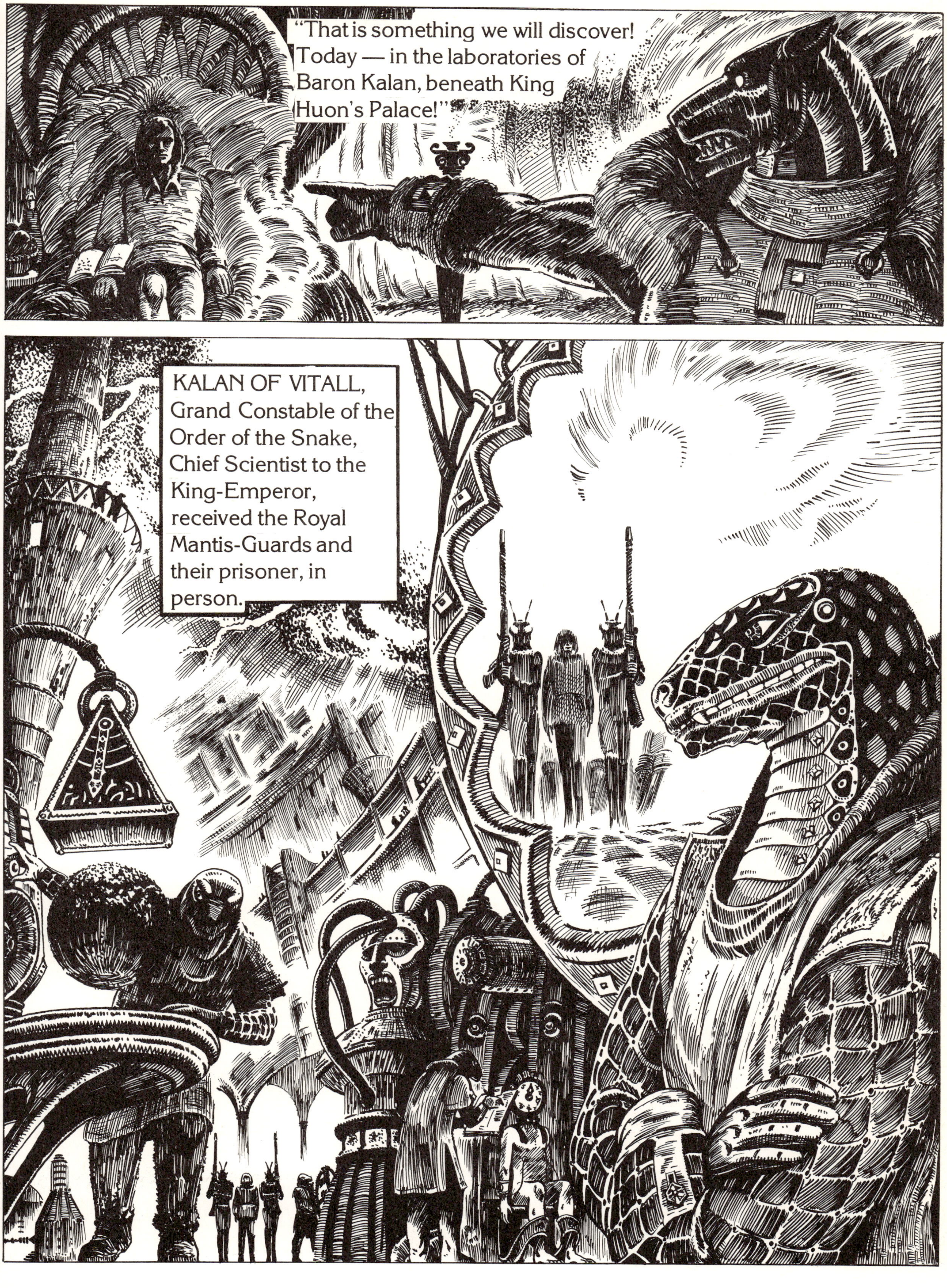

KALAN OF VITALL, Grand Constable of the Order of the Snake, Chief Scientist to the King-Emperor, received the Royal Mantis-Guards and their prisoner, in person.

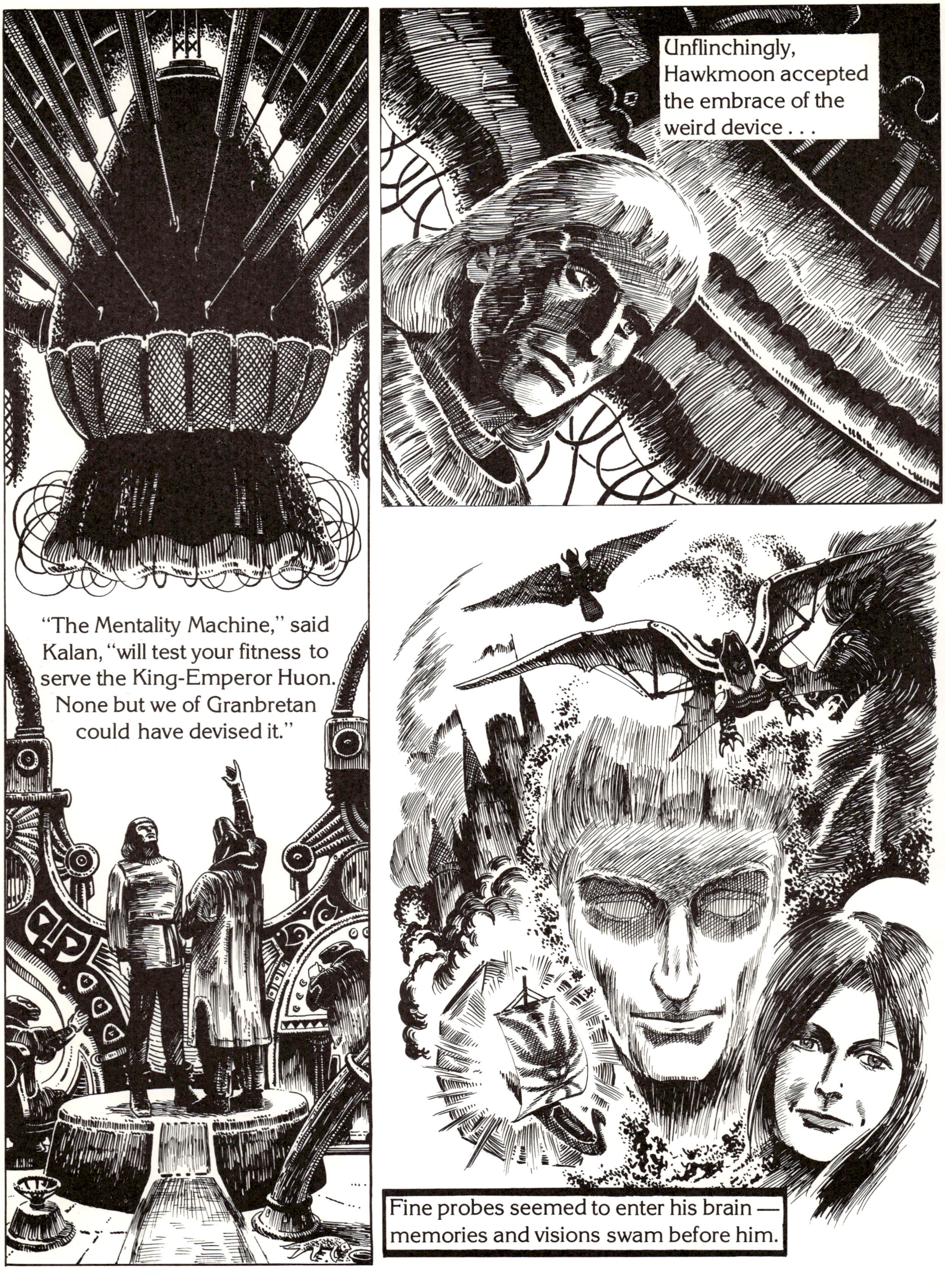

"The Mentality Machine," said Kalan, "will test your fitness to serve the King-Emperor Huon. None but we of Granbretan could have devised it."

He was assailed by swordsmen and strange beasts . . . calmly, unemotionally, Hawkmoon outfought them all.
The Machine withdrew. "Interesting, my Lord Duke," whispered Kalan. "In some peculiar way, you are too sane."
In Kalan's chambers, they drank a strange, strong wine. "My own invention — not grapes, but GRAIN!"
"Sanity — who can truly judge it? Some say — ha, ha! — that it is we of Granbretan who are mad!"
Irony stirred briefly in Hawkmoon as the fiery spirit took effect. "Surely not . . ."

"Baron Kalan finds your psyche . . . enigmatic. Yet I require a service, and would bargain with you. Count Brass of the Kamarg opposes our will. But he would not suspect the Hero of Köln."

"You wish me to go to the Kamarg?"
"Yes — you will seek refuge with Count Brass. You will abduct his daughter — Yisselda. For her sake, he must do whatever we demand. In return, you can go back to Köln, as ruler of your people!"

"I will do as you ask. Why not?"

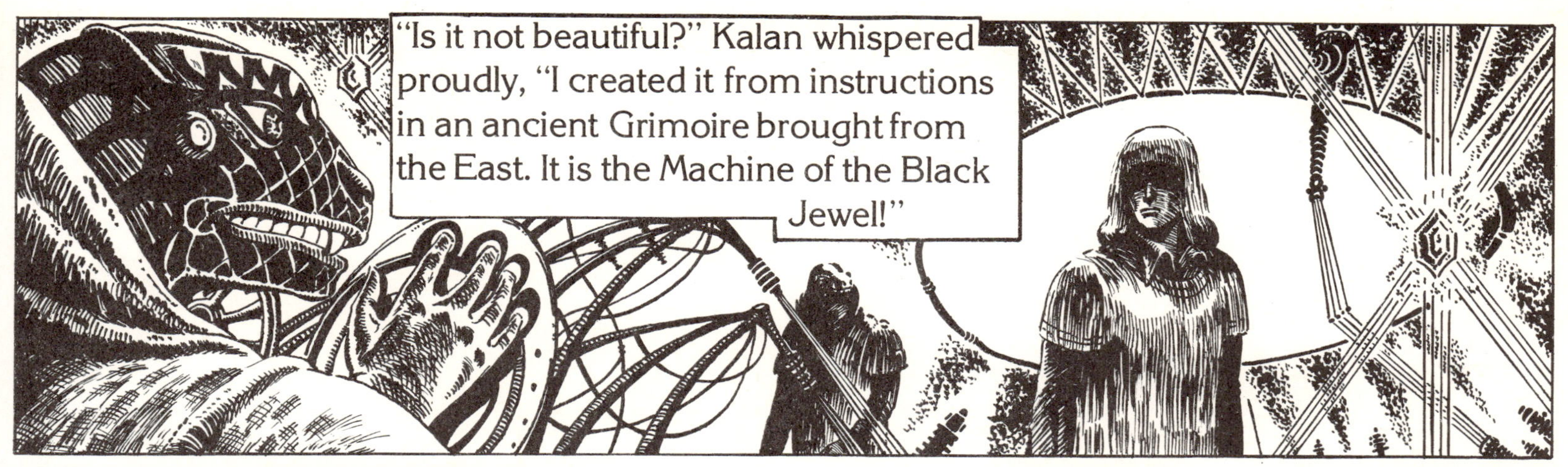

"THROUGH IT, WE SEE WHATEVER YOUR OWN EYES SEE. AND IF YOU BETRAY US, WE WILL GIVE THE JEWEL ITS FULL LIFE . . .

AND IT WILL EAT YOUR BRAIN!"

BETWEEN THE RANKS OF MANTIS-GUARDS WITH READY FLAME-LANCES, BETWEEN THE MURMURING CROWDS OF COURTIERS AND PETITIONERS, HAWKMOON AND MELIADUS PACED TO AN AUDIENCE WITH THE IMMORTAL KING-EMPEROR, HUON.

A half-mile beyond the great doors, they prostrated themselves before the Throne-Globe. From within the golden mesh of her Heron-mask, COUNTESS FLANA OF KANBERY, only living relative of the King-Emperor, watched with a faint curiosity. Wife of the Muskovian mercenary, Asrovak Mikosevaar, she had once been married to Meliadus.
Above her, Huon spoke: "Baron Meliadus, we go to much effort to secure the services of Count Brass. Can we trust this Duke von Köln?"
"The Jewel ensures his loyalty, Immortal Ruler," Meliadus said.

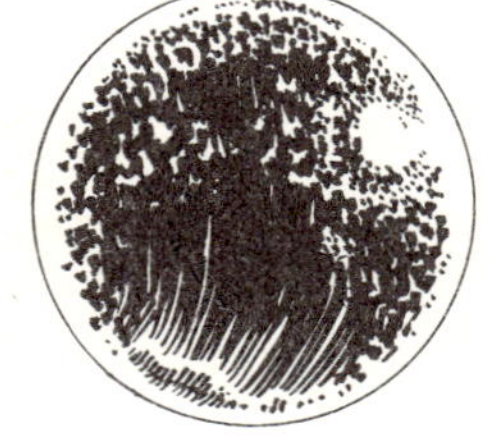

The Throne-Globe darkened. As Hawkmoon turned away, some buried part of his mind that had stirred faintly beneath the probing of the Mentality-Machine, awoke again.

Perhaps, this time, the stimulus came from elsewhere . . .

Beyond the prison gates, Hawkmoon boarded a steel and silver ornithopter.

THE GRIFFIN CLIMBED, PITCHING AND SWAYING, METAL WINGS THRASHING. HAWKMOON CLOSED HIS EYES, SHUTTING OUT THE ROCKING SKY. WHEN HE OPENED THEM AGAIN, HE WAS OVER DEAU-VERE. FROM HERE SPRANG THE SILVER BRIDGE THAT BORE THE ARMIES OF GRANBRETAN MARCHING AGAINST EUROPE.
TO HAWKMOON'S INTENSE RELIEF, THE BALANCE OF HIS JOURNEY WOULD BE ON HORSEBACK.

He rode into Europe, passing the incoming spoils of a plundered continent.

Sleeping at an inn, he woke during the night and saw a warrior armoured in jet and gold.

Hawkmoon forgot the apparition as he rode South, where the Standards of Granbretan marked their conquests.

Wolf and Serpent studied the Quartz Slab which reflected the vision of the Black Jewel. "Aah . . . he approaches our forward lines, in the fields of Lyon!"

The madness of
the Dark Empire
blossomed in the
blackened meadows.

In the lands beyond
Lyon which were still
free, soldiers hailed
him as a hero.

The real test, however, lay
ahead in the wind-whipped,
lonely Kamarg.

IT SEEMED THAT COUNT BRASS, THE WISE BOWGENTLE AND THE FOLK OF THE CASTLE ACCEPTED HIM AS A WARRIOR SEEKING REST AND REFUGE. YISSELDA'S AFFECTIONATE NATURE RESPONDED TO HIS SOMBRE SPIRIT.

Bowgentle recited new verses of his own composition, elegant, witty, full of strange rhythms.

Soon, Hawkmoon ceased to be aware of anything but the poet's voice and gestures.

He tried to rise, to speak, then fell forward, unconscious.

"Your rhymes have worked well, old friend," said Count Brass. "Now we must act quickly, before the watchers in Londra become suspicious."

Out of sight of the Black Jewel, Count Brass said: "We probed your mind while you slept. Your mission was an evil one, but the evil was not yours. You are a victim of Granbretan's sorcery, and we would save you. Bowgentle will be here soon. Go with him."

Chatting lightly to lull Londra's lip reading watchers, Bowgentle led the way to the study of Count Brass.

Hawkmoon followed Bowgentle into darkness. Then, suddenly — !

He woke with a tremendous feeling of well-being. The Jewel no longer pulsed with life, but was hard and cold beneath his fingers.
"It had to be done quickly, without warning Granbretan," Count Brass explained.
"But I cannot constrain the Jewel for long . . . six months, a year, not more."

"Malagigi of Hamadan might have the skill to remove the Jewel," Bowgentle said.
"Hamadan? It is a long journey to Persia. Perhaps too long . . ."

As he recovered, he was often with Yisselda, exploring the wide, wild Kamarg.

"Will you go, then, to Persia?" she asked. He brushed aside her wind-tangled hair . . .

"I have a new life, an unforeseen life. There are new decisions to make."

"Reports say that Granbretan's forces are marching directly South.
I fear this change of tactics is aimed at the Kamarg."

"Let them come! We can resist them at any point."

"Why allow them to choose their ground? We can divert their attack to where we are strongest!"

N
W
E
S
AIGUES MORTES
"Here, where our Towers are on high hills, and the marshes are deep. With two hundred warriors, I can drive their army as a dog drives cattle!"

Two weeks later, Hawkmoon's heavily-armed riders saw the full might of the Dark Empire.

WOLF-MASKED MELIADUS RODE BESIDE THE RUTHLESS MERCENARY, ASROVAK MIKOSEVAAR, LORD OF THE VULTURE LEGION. BEHIND THEM FLUTTERED THE STANDARDS OF A HUNDRED CAPTAINS OF GRANBRETAN. BUT HAWKMOON LOOKED BEYOND THEM TO THE RIVER, AND SMILED . . .

A day's ride beyond the army, an ancient bridge spanned the River Rhone . . .
"The piers have decayed. Concentrate your fire here . . . and here . . ."
The Flame-Lances burned!
Rubble choked the River, forcing the waters into new channels.

As the sun sank, the Dark Empire commanders surveyed a scene of chaos. Deprived of their supply barges, the marching columns ground to a halt. When camp had been made, and the cursing soldiers were labouring to save their supplies from the shrunken Rhone, Hawkmoon struck!

The riders of the Kamarg tore through the lightly-guarded camp, burning and killing. They came to the Mantis Standard of King Huon . . .
"HAWKMOON!"
"My thanks, Baron, for the care you took of me in Londra!"
Hawkmoon drew back his arm for the death-stroke —
— but the burning Mantis Standard fell between them. He retreated before a swarm of Dark Empire soldiery.

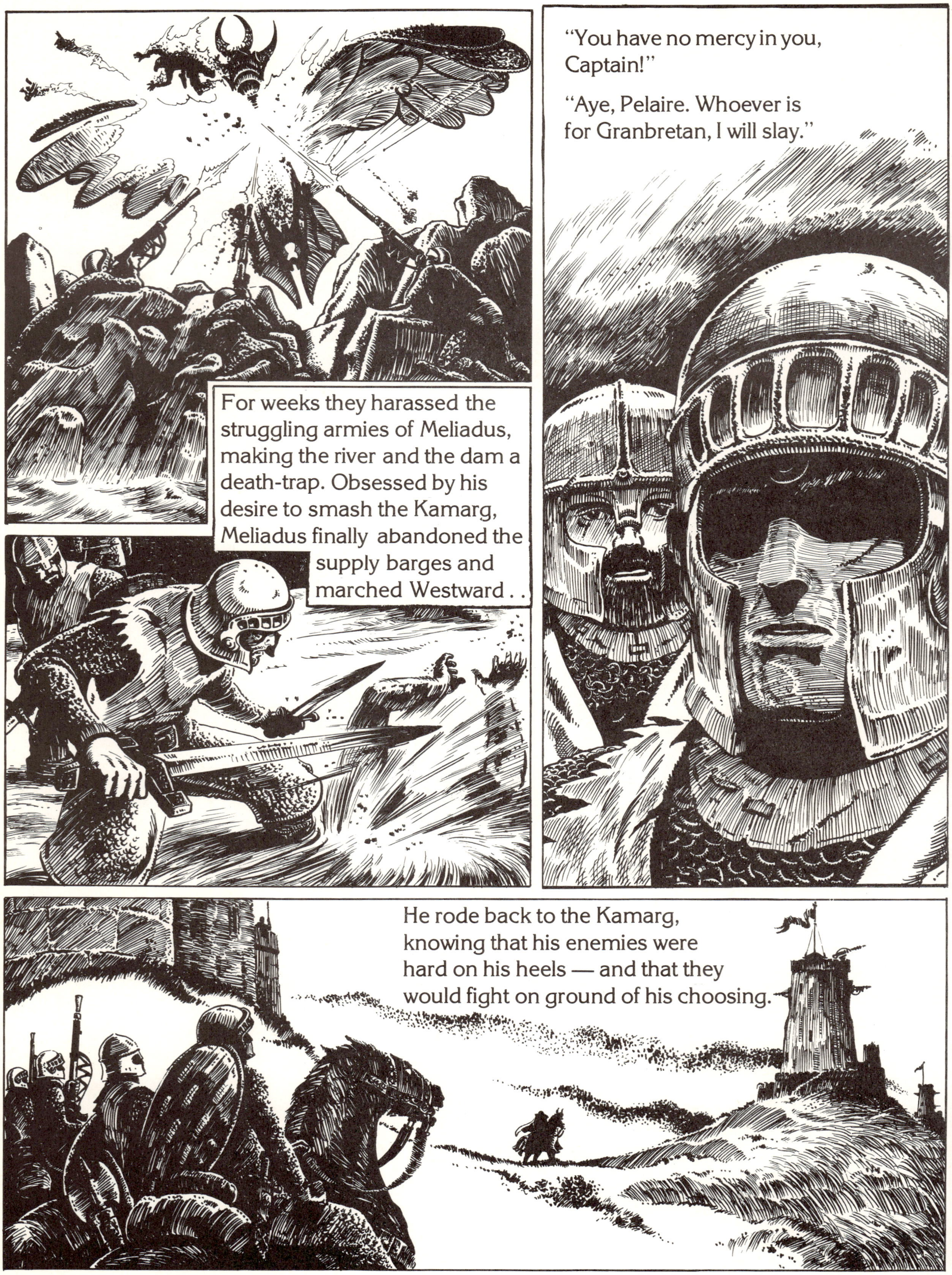

For weeks they harassed the struggling armies of Meliadus, making the river and the dam a death-trap. Obsessed by his desire to smash the Kamarg, Meliadus finally abandoned the supply barges and marched Westward . .

"You have no mercy in you, Captain!"

"Aye, Pelaire. Whoever is for Granbretan, I will slay."

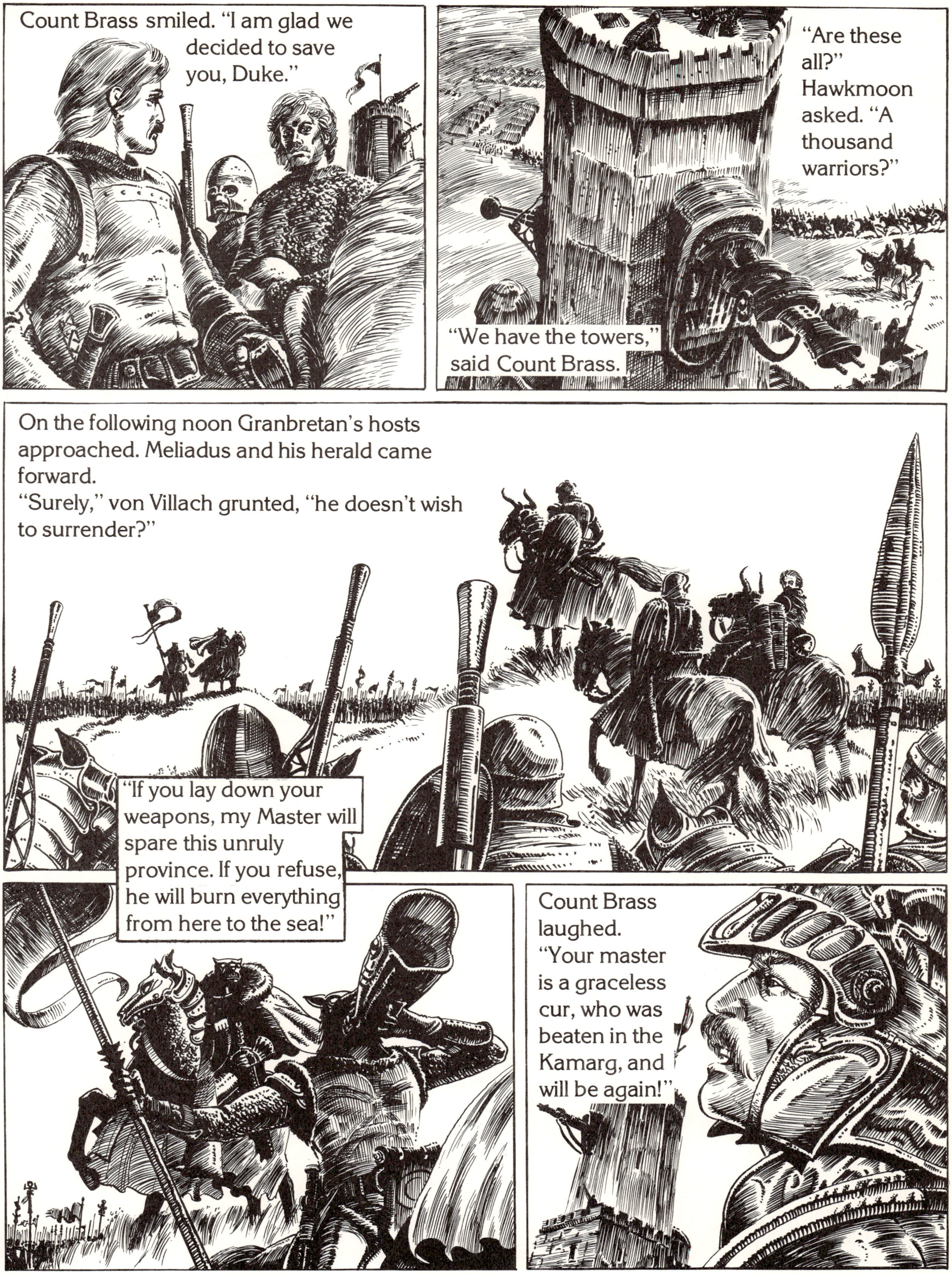

On the following noon Granbretan's hosts approached. Meliadus and his herald came forward.
"Surely," von Villach grunted, "he doesn't wish to surrender?"

"If you lay down your weapons, my Master will spare this unruly province. If you refuse, he will burn everything from here to the sea!"

Count Brass laughed. "Your master is a graceless cur, who was beaten in the Kamarg, and will be again!"

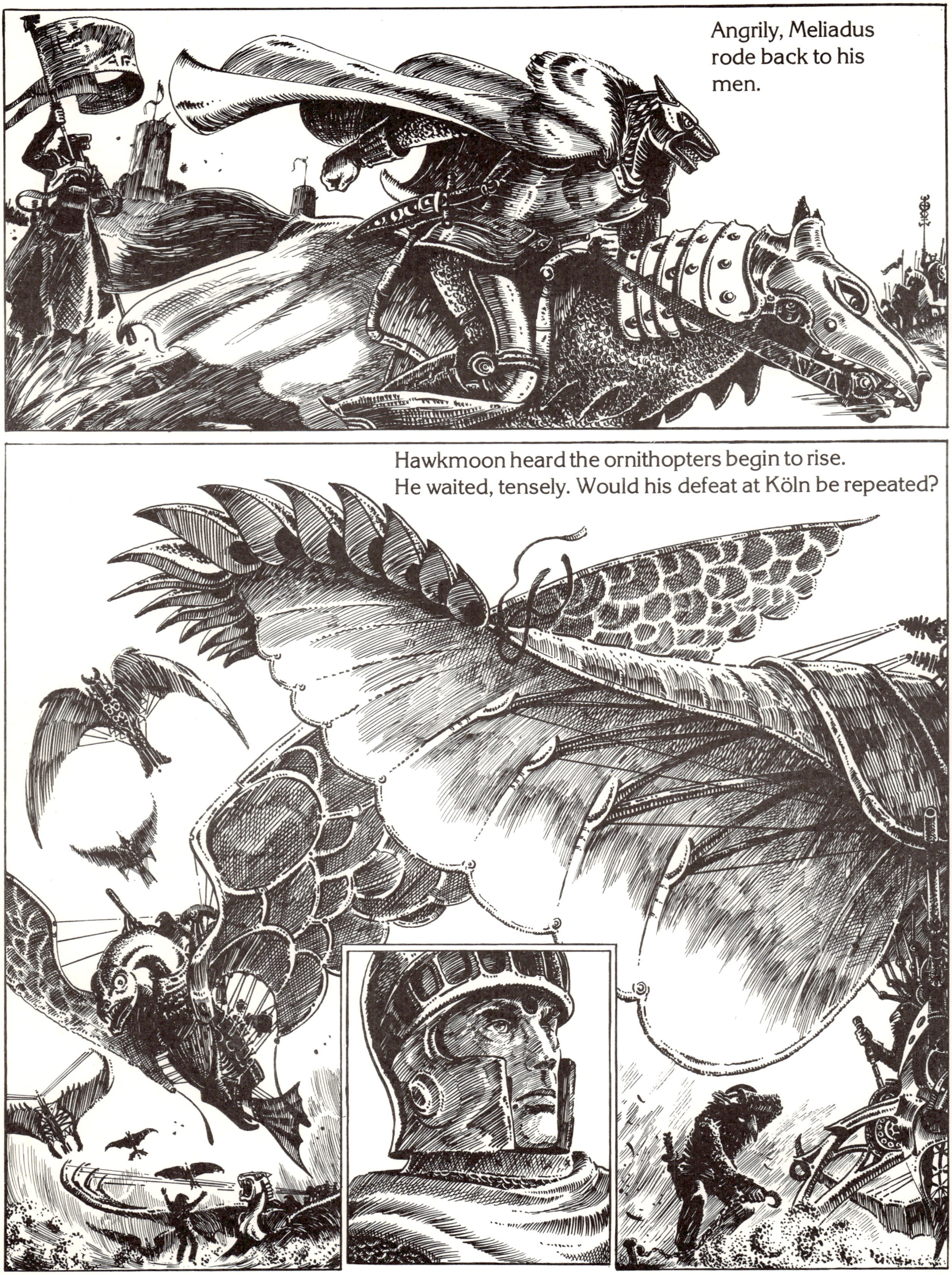

Hawkmoon heard the ornithopters begin to rise.
He waited, tensely. Would his defeat at Köln be repeated?

He had not reckoned on the
flamingoes: they swept up from
the Towers in scarlet clouds:
Flame-lances blazed!

Hard behind the ornithopters came the Dark Empire cavalry, line upon armoured line. "Towers — open fire!" yelled Count Brass.

Tight beams of sound
shrieked from the
jutting nozzles. The
charging horses reared,
bucked and fell.

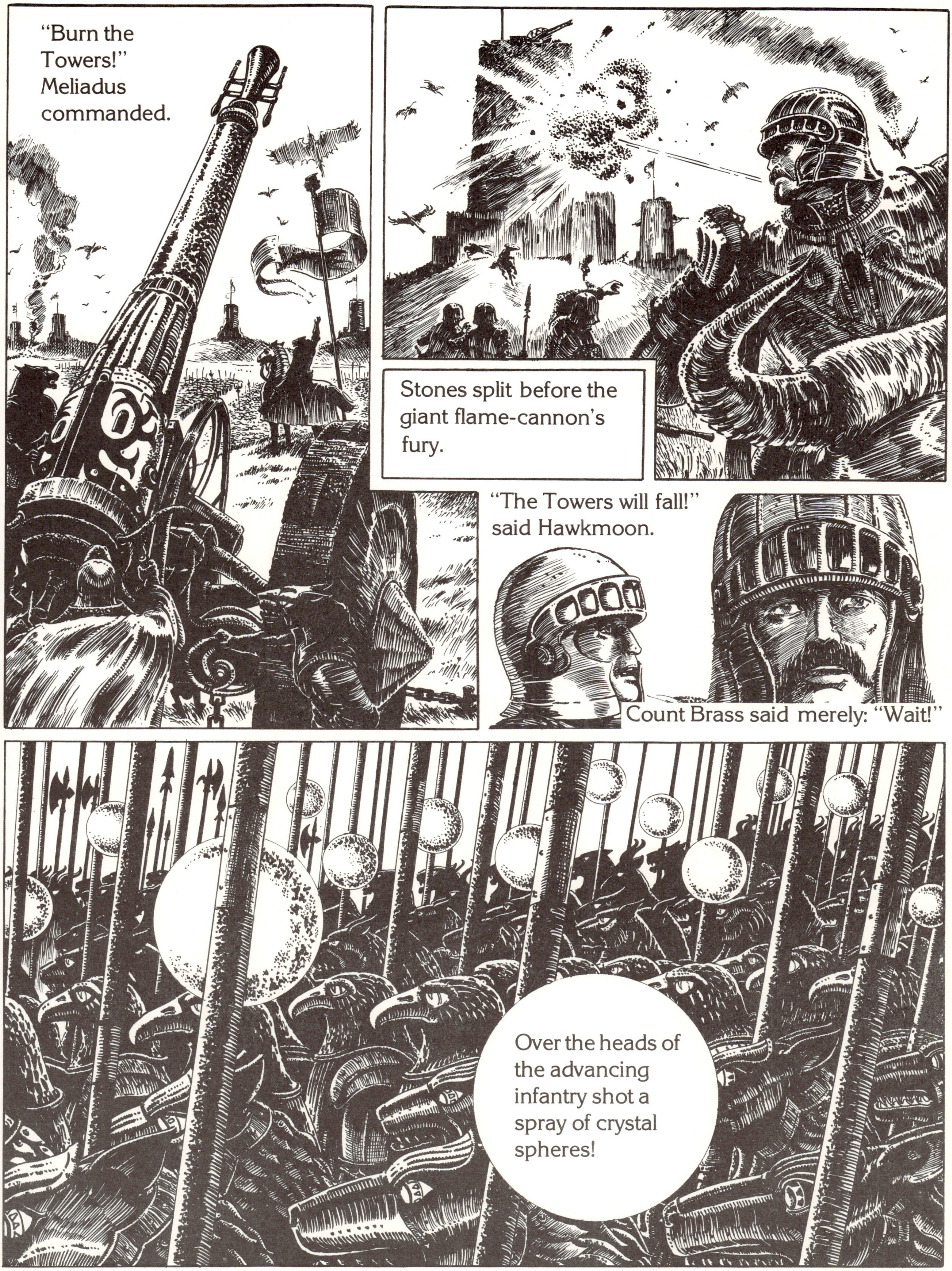

"The Towers will fall!" said Hawkmoon.

Count Brass said merely: "Wait!"

Over the heads of the advancing infantry shot a spray of crystal spheres!

Shattering, the spheres released hallucinatory gasses. Terrifying visions filled the minds of the Granbretanians.

NOW THE KAMARGIANS CLASHED WITH THEIR DISORGANISED FOES, AS THE DISCIPLINE OF THE DARK EMPIRE TROOPS BEGAN TO CRUMBLE. HAWKMOON DISMOUNTED TO CONFRONT VULTURE-MASKED
ASROVAK MIKOSEVAAR.

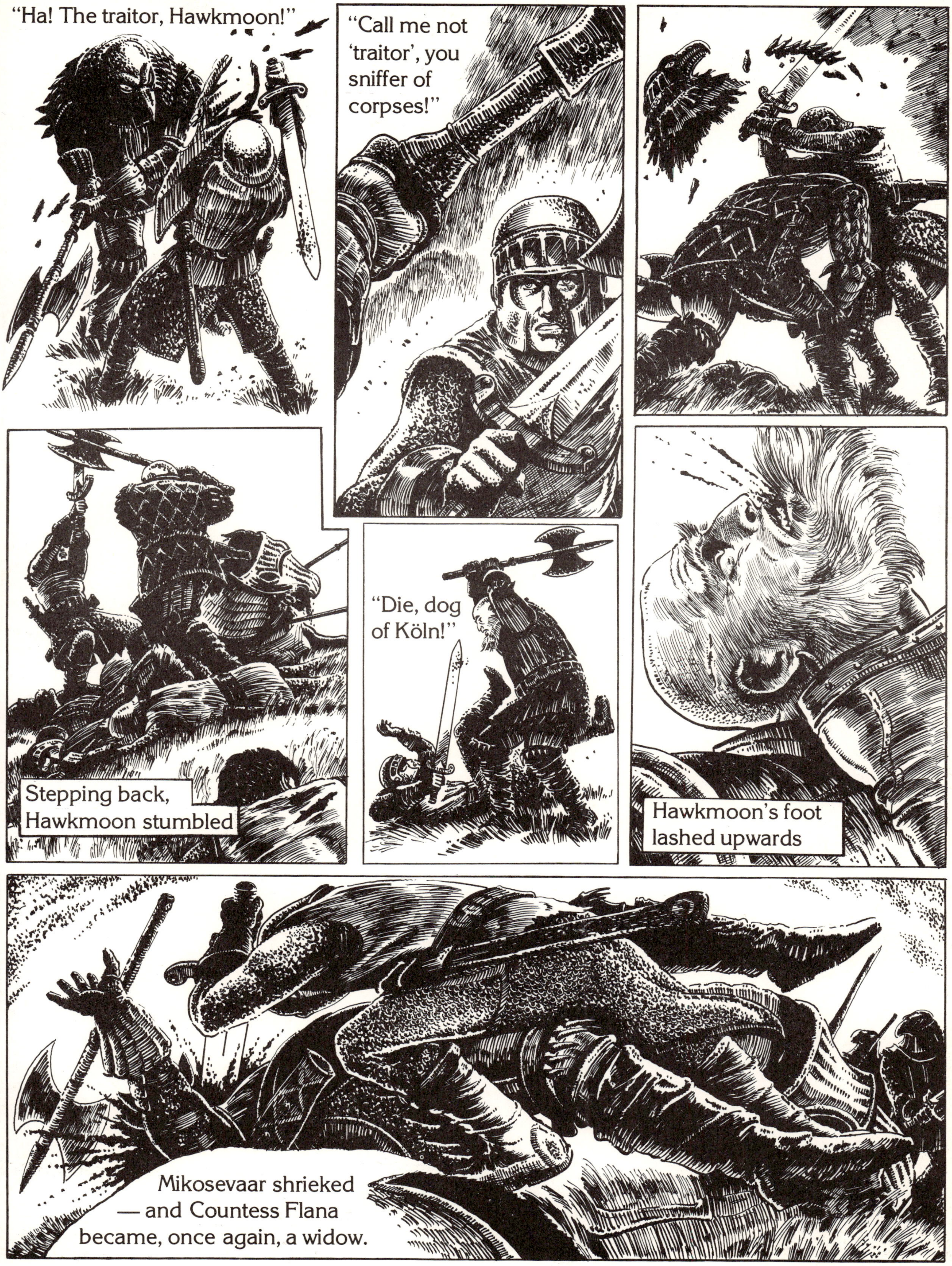

"Ha! The traitor, Hawkmoon!"

"Call me not 'traitor', you sniffer of corpses!"

Stepping back, Hawkmoon stumbled

"Die, dog of Köln!"

Hawkmoon's foot lashed upwards

The remnants of Meliadus's huge army broke and fled. Ruthlessly, the Kamarg cavalry rode them down. "You seem resolved to destroy Granbretan single-handed, my friend," said von Villach.

"Stay!" Count Brass ordered. "They have lost their taste for our blood."

On the ravaged plain, Meliadus gave way
to his weary captains and signalled
retreat. His wordless scream of
rage carried faintly to the
ears of Hawkmoon . . .

There was little talk on the long ride back to Castle Brass.

"Do you see now, Count, that Granbretan is a danger to all of humanity?" Bowgentle asked. "I agree," said Hawkmoon. "They are more than conquerors."

"There is an insanity in them, a hostility directed not only at their enemies, but at life itself.

Count Brass sighed. "Perhaps you are right. Only the Runestaff could tell."

Hawkmoon rose. "Where is Yisselda?" "She sleeps, I think." said Bowgentle.

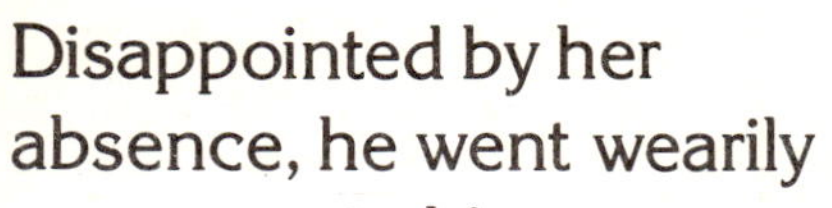

"You love me, Dorian. Why do you deny it?" "I must" Hawkmoon said. "For your sake. Soon, the Black Jewel will destroy me!"

She listened to the tale of his bargain with the Lords of Granbretan.

". . . and to search for Malagigi," he ended, "may take whatever time remains to me."

DORIAN HAWKMOON FLEW EAST TO DISTANT PERSIA

SEEKING THE SORCERER MALAGIGI. IN HIS FOREHEAD, THE BLACK JEWEL PULSED WITH RETURNING LIFE, EMPHASISING THE URGENCY OF HIS MISSION. THE GIANT SCARLET BIRD BORE HIM SWIFTLY AND EASILY, AND AFTER SEVEN DAYS HE WAS CROSSING A RANGE OF MOUNTAINS FAR BEYOND THE KAMARG. DUSK WAS FALLING. AS THE FLAMINGO BEGAN A SWEEPING DESCENT, HAWKMOON SAW A PARTY OF MEN BELOW.

The flamingo screamed!

Above the dazed Hawkmoon, someone said: "Is he a warlock? That Jewel . . ."

"They say the Granbretanians wish revenge upon such a man. They offer gold."

"Then we will take just enough evidence to — AAGH!"

As the second arrow struck, Hawkmoon surged into life.

"So the rumours have run ahead of me? How far has the Dark Empire reached?"

As they roasted his late steed, Hawkmoon told his story to the sympathetic Olahdan. "Tomorrow I will obtain riding beasts," the little giant promised. "They are goats, but large."

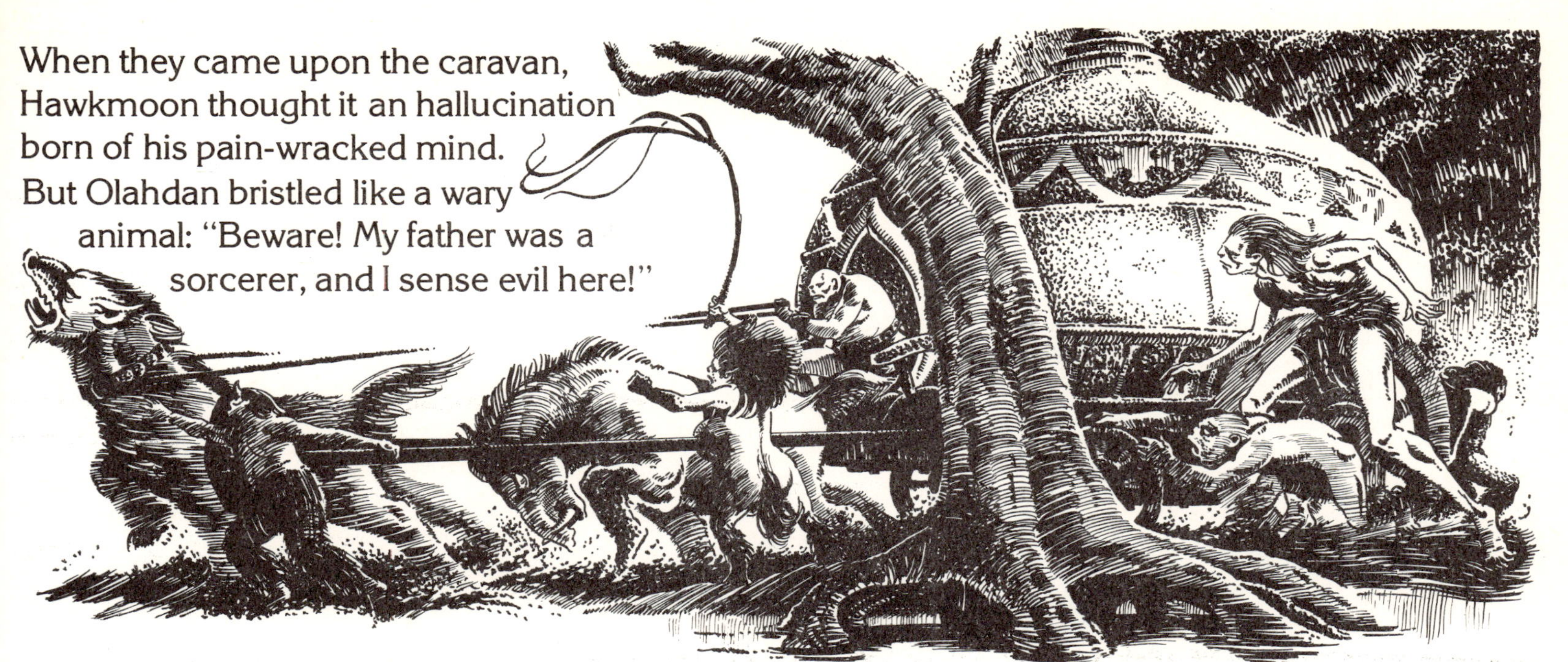
When they came upon the caravan,
Hawkmoon thought it an hallucination
born of his pain-wracked mind.
But Olahdan bristled like a wary
animal: "Beware! My father was a
sorcerer, and I sense evil here!"

Hawkmoon gasped.
"That is the caravan of
Agonosvos, banished
from Köln nine
centuries ago!"

"You are ill, Duke
Dorian. My wine will
ease your pain."
"Yes, I still live,"
whispered Agonosvos.
"Your ancestors
forfeited my loyalty, but I
make you welcome,
last Duke of Köln."

"Do not drink!" shouted Olahdan. "The wine is drugged!"

Agonosvos voiced a weird cry —
beast-men leaped into the caravan.

"Hold!" said Hawkmoon. "I am Duke of Köln and therefore still your Lord!"

Agonosvos laughed. "Take these fools!"

As Agonosvos fell, the beast-men fled.
Outside, Hawkmoon pointed to a pair of magnificent blue horses. "We'll saddle those and be on our way!"

A bolt of agony seared through his brain, pitching him headlong.

Aghast, they glared up at Agonosvos.
"You abuse my hospitality, Duke of Köln.

Perhaps you prefer that of Baron Meliadus. We are old allies, Granbretan and I.
The Baron will pay a rare price for your living body. My agents foresaw your coming, and I sent word to him."

Olahdan sprang, clawing at the black helm!

"NO-OO-O!"

On the fine blue horses, they rode to the Mermian Sea.

As a merchantman bore them East to the coast of Tarkia, Hawkmoon saw distant sails in close formation.

"Dark Empire ships" growled the Captain. "The sea is thick with them."

Many dusty leagues later, they saw the walls of Hamadan — and the fires of battle! Out from the gates poured an army in retreat. At sight of them, the leader reined in.

A trembling looter directed them to Malagigi's house.

"Gods!" Olahdan cried. "We are too late!"

Hopelessly the house-guards struck at the monster.

Hawkmoon hurled himself over the locked gates.

Driven by pain and despair, he slashed madly at the devil-beast.

"I am Malagigi" the man said. "Thank you, warrior. I was not prepared for such powerful sorcery."
Hawkmoon panted, "I seek your help against Granbretan. The Jewel I bear is also their work."

"The wars of the West do not concern me. I will do nothing for either faction."

"Damn you, sorcerer! Without your aid, the Jewel will destroy me — and Granbretan will destroy Hamadan!"

"If you are truly a victim of Granbretan," Malagigi said, "prove it to me by driving them from the city."

"I will return, sorcerer!" Hawkmoon yelled wildly.

Barely had they left, when: "Tell your Master Malagigi that the Baron Meliadus commands his presence!"

Queen Frawbra had retreated into the hills. And there Hawkmoon saw the armoured figure of his visions. "So Malagigi would not help you?"
"Who are you? How do you know ?"

"I am The Warrior in Jet and Gold."

"The Queen's brother Nahak is in league with Meliadus", said the deep rich voice. "Your only hope is to join forces to retake Hamadan."

"Would you try?" Hawkmoon said.
"Aye", said Queen Frawbra, "if my men will follow me."

"Majesty — the last of our men to leave the city say that the westerners have imprisoned Malagigi!"

"If Malagigi is in Meliadus's hands, there is no hope for me . . ."

"Nonsense! Soon it will be dark. They will not expect a counter-attack. And what have you to lose?"

FRAWBRA'S MEN RALLIED BEHIND THEIR STRANGE NEW ALLIES. THE HAUNTED, WHITE-FACED INTENSITY OF HAWKMOON FILLED THEM WITH AN ALMOST SUPERSTITIOUS AWE: THEY STORMED INTO SLEEPING HAMADAN, RIDING DOWN THE DRUNKEN, DAZED SOLDIERS WHO FACED THEM.

Meliadus and Nahak held the Palace Square.
"Where is the traitor, Hawkmoon?"
shouted the Baron.

"Here, Meliadus, to destroy you!"

"Destroy me? At my command, the Jewel will kill you — unless you order your men to surrender!"

Sudden agony made Hawkmoon reel.

"Lord Dorian, I kept the helmet of Agonosvos for such a time as this.
Wear it now!"

"It can shield you from the Jewel's power for a short while."
Shuddering, Hawkmoon donned the Black Helm.

The pain faded. He laughed —

— and yelled "Charge!"

"Curse you, Hawkmoon!"

Bewildered, Nahak raised his shield . . .

. . . but too late.
"Die, brother!"

Hawkmoon felt his horse stumble —

— a blow from Meliadus drove
him out of the saddle.

He sprang up, ducking
beneath the Baron's
descending blade, and —

"AAGGH!"

He dragged the dazed warlord from his horse!

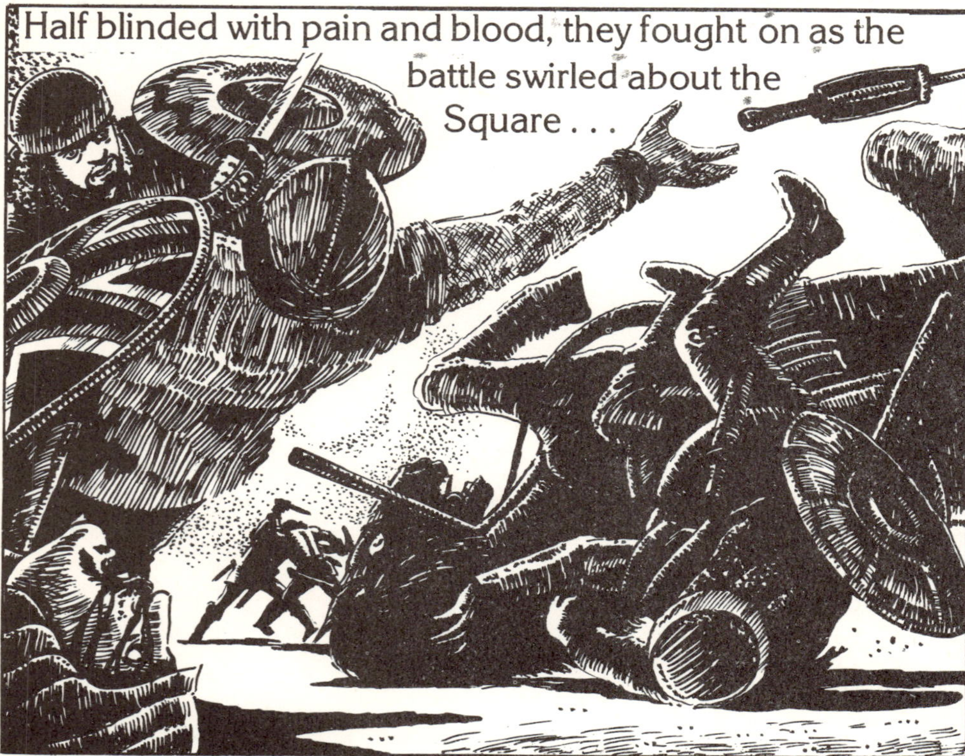
Half blinded with pain and blood, they fought on as the battle swirled about the Square . . .

. . . just before dawn, searchers came looking for the living.

"Quickly," Olahdan said, "take him to Malagigi. Leave the Granbretanian's body."

CONSCIOUSNESS RETURNED TO HAWKMOON, YET HE WAS UNAWARE OF THE WORLD AROUND HIM. PEACEFULLY, HE DRIFTED AMID MISTY, EVER-CHANGING COLOURS. THEN VEINS OF BLOOD-RED WOVE THROUGH THE PASTEL HUES . . . THERE WAS BLACKNESS, AND A WRENCHING PAIN . . .

HE SCREAMED!

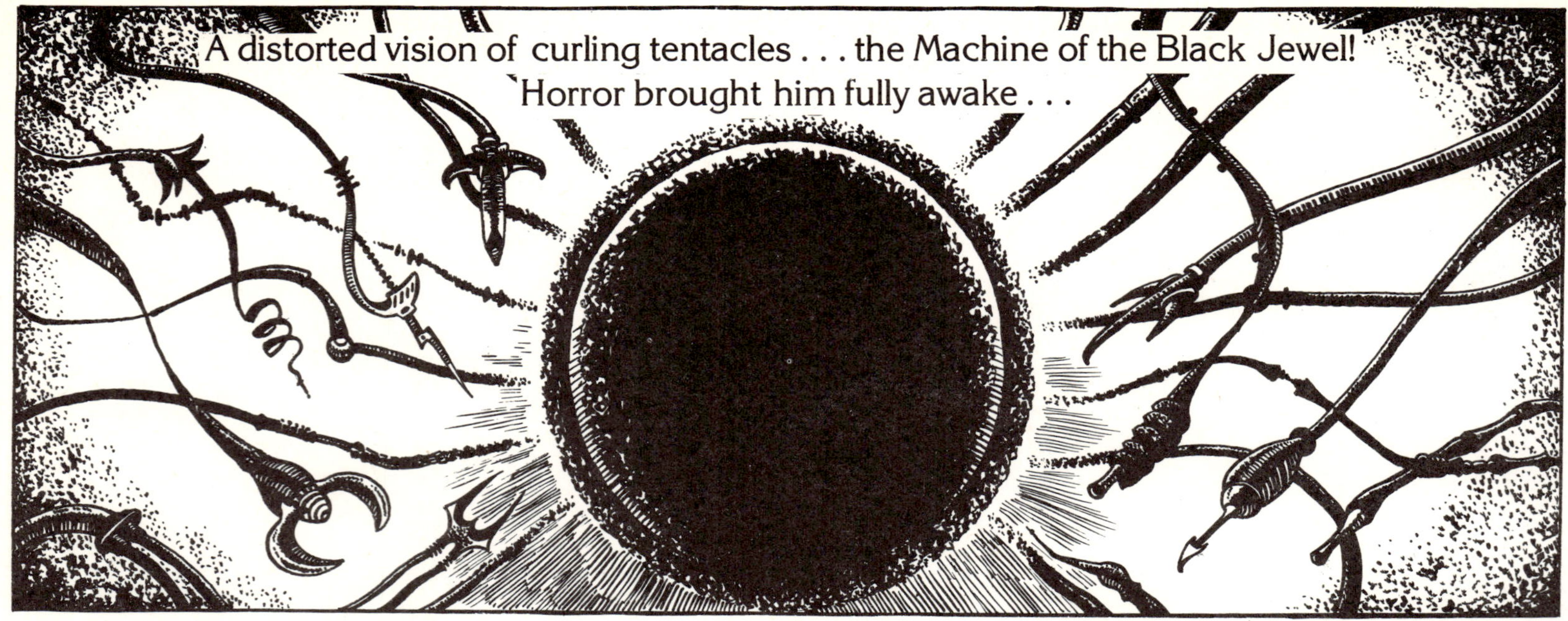
A distorted vision of curling tentacles . . . the Machine of the Black Jewel!
Horror brought him fully awake . . .

"Who . . . Malagigi! How did you get the Machine?"

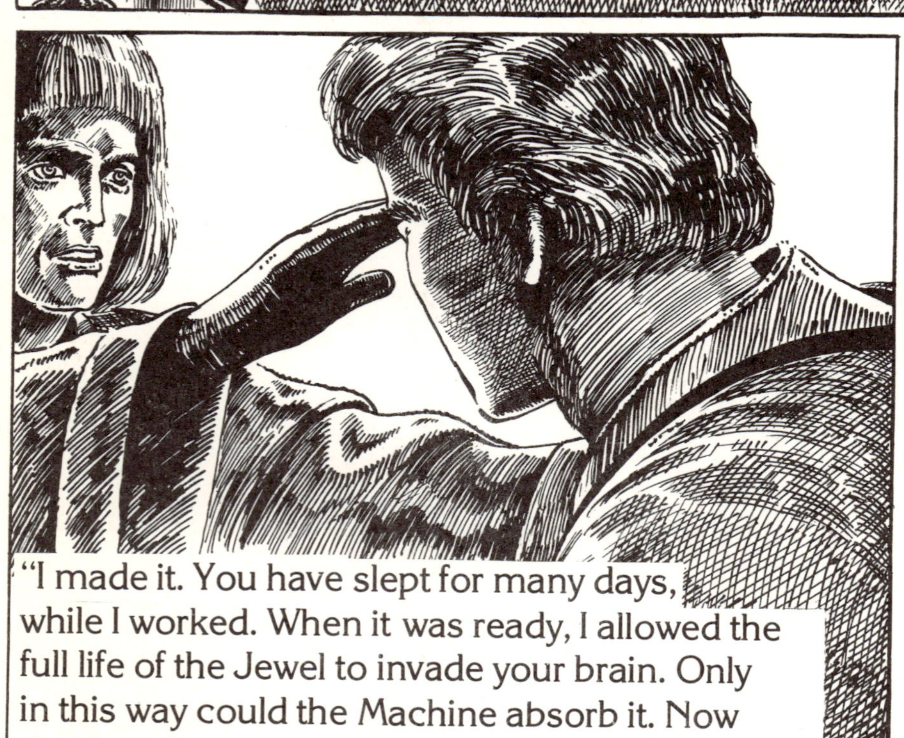
"I made it. You have slept for many days, while I worked. When it was ready, I allowed the full life of the Jewel to invade your brain. Only in this way could the Machine absorb it. Now the Jewel is dead. If you wish, I can remove it . . ."

"Yes, it is truly dead. But I will wear it as a symbol of my hatred: until Granbretan is destroyed!"

Later, Hawkmoon said: "I thank you, Malagigi. And you also, Warrior. Perhaps we will meet again."

"Perhaps, for the warrior told me that we serve the same power.
It was for that reason I killed the Black Jewel."

"You told Malagigi that we serve the same power, and so saved my life. What Power?"

"I serve the Runestaff," said the warrior in Jet and Gold.

"The Runestaff?" Olahdan said. "A myth, surely?" Hawkmoon laughed. Let's to more important matters — what of Meliadus?"

"When we returned to pick up his body, his men had borne it away." "So my greatest enemy is dead? What better news could I carry when I return to wed Yisselda!"

AND SO DORIAN HAWKMOON, DUKE OF KÖLN, RODE WESTWARD WITH OLAHDAN, TO CLAIM HIS LOVE AND TAKE HIS VENGEANCE UPON THE DARK EMPIRE.

The story of Dorian Hawkmoon will be continued in Volume Two of the High History of the Runestaff, entitled:
"THE MAD GOD'S AMULET."

JAMES CAWTHORN

Interviewed by David Britton

James Cawthorn (left) with David Britton. Circa 1973.

Satellite (Ed Don Allen), cover, circa 1957 – Modelled on the general design of the covers of **Planet Stories** from the early fifties.

David Britton: Can we begin at the beginning? Where was your work first published?

James Cawthorn: SATELLITE, published by Don Allen, was the fanzine which first published my work. I met Don in 1953, so it would be either 1953/4 that I got in touch with a lot more fanzines through **SATELLITE,** and eventually found one advertising two Edgar Rice Burroughs fanzines, one by Peter Ogden **(ERBANIA)** in Blackpool, and one by Mike Moorcock **(BURROUGHSANIA)** in London. This would be in 1956, so I wrote off to both of them and ended up by illustrating both, and I still keep in regular touch with Peter Ogden, although he's now living in Florida. He still publishes **ERBANIA** regularly, and I still appear in most issues.

D.B: And from illustrating the Michael Moorcock fanzine you eventually began to appear in **TARZAN ADVENTURES?**

J.C: Very shortly after I met Mike, when he was about seventeen I think, he got offered the editorship of **TA,** and he began looking around for new artists because he had a totally different policy in mind to the one that had been used for **TA** until then. The man who had been running the magazine was fairly elderly and at that time he had a rather mild, 'Children's Hour' approach to his readership, and Mike wanted to move the magazine up into the teenage bracket and higher. So he rounded up a lot of people to write and draw. He reprinted some of the artwork I had done off my own bat, for no particular market, and in or around 1956/57 I began to illustrate the **Sojan** tales of his which he serialised in **TA.**

D.B: How much later did you become involved in the **SEXTON BLAKE LIBRARY?**

J.C: When Mike eventually left **TARZAN ADVENTURES** and went to work for IPC. He ended up on the **SEXTON BLAKE LIBRARY** with Howard Baker, and again they used quite a few different artists for the interior illustrations. These were very small drawings about one-inch-and-a-half by half-an-inch when printed. Incidentally I worked with Mike on a Sexon Blake novel called **Caribbean Crisis** which I believe they published under a pseudonym around 1960 and is now a much sought after book.

D.B: Can you remember if you did any for Jack Trevor Story's Sexton Blake novels?

J.C: I don't think I did anything specifically for Jack Trevor Story, but it's quite likely they could have reprinted some for his Blake novels.

D.B: Around the time you were illustrating the **Sojan** tales in **TA** you began to write your own **Sword and Sorcery** series, **Handar the Red.**

J.C: Well, I wrote one story which was published in **TA** in three parts, yet everybody insists on referring to it as a series! I also wrote a couple of articles as far as I can remember, and I did a four-episode comic strip, **Peril Planet,** which Mike had commissioned as a five-episode strip, and he was rather disappointed when he found it ended up only having four.

D.B: You had experimented with comic strips prior to **Peril Planet.** Do you still have those original strips?

J.C: You mean the Conan strip? Yes, I still have them. I did the Conan strip around 1953/54. I did a lot of strip work at that time, but this was not done commercially of course. I did two Conan stories at least, but I never really completed either of them. I did several Edgar Rice Burroughs strips, **Gods of Mars, Warlord of Mars, Pellucidar,** and **The Land That Time Forgot.** That was largely why I ended up working on the film script for **The Land That Time Forgot** in the early '70s, because I had already done a breakdown of it several years before, and since breaking down a story for a strip cartoon is pretty similar to breaking it down for film script.

D.B: Who were your early influences?

J.C: In the late 1940s I was heavily influenced by such people as Milton Caniff and Burne Hogarth, because the magazine **Canadian Star Weekly** was still on sale in this country at that time, and it carried all the colour Sunday strips. I read this for a couple of years, and as I say I was very influenced at that time by their style.

D.B: You recently met Hogarth. Do you feel that his work suffers in any way by comparison with his late 1940s strip work?

J.C: Yes, I think quite a good deal of it does. I think the first Tarzan hardbound book did not match up to the Sunday strips. But his later Tarzan book, **Jungle Tales of Tarzan,** appears to have redressed the balance. He seems to have come back on form again.

D.B: What do you think of Hogarth's latest project, the book of King Arthur?

J.C: It will be interesting. But the point is that people are always wanting him to do things other than the things that he wants to do himself, and at the meeting we had with him the other day he explained quite clearly what his philosophy is. I can see now why various characters such as John Carter of Mars, or Conan, which he seemed better fitted for than practically any other artist I can think of, simply do not fit in with his philosophy or his moral outlook, and don't appeal to him at all. So we will probably never see any of this by him, which is a great pity. Hogarth does appear to have this belief that everything should be 'onward and upward', and does not want to support the general air of doom and destruction and world-ending that Howard went in for.

Burroughsania, No.18, 1958 – Typical Cawthorn cover for Michael Moorcock's Edgar Rice Burroughs fanzine.

Erbania (Ed Peter Ogden), interior, circa 1958 – A stencil illustration from Robert E. Howard's **Valley of the Worm.**

D.B: Which is very much at odds with the atmosphere of doomed hysteria that permeates much of his Tarzan strips.

J.C: Yes, his own artwork is full of latent violence and destruction which is what makes it attractive. But he appears to think that that's been channelled into constructive uses.

D.B: Could you tell me when you first met Mervyn Peake?

J.C: I had been to Mervyn's home sometime in the late 1950s, but he was extremely ill and it was difficult to visualise what he must have been like when he was in his prime. He had a very impressive face. Even his illness had not diluted this effect. He had the kind of face that artists are supposed to have, you know, the burning eyes, et cetera, but he couldn't talk very much, or at least it was quite an effort for him to talk. He was quite coherent and rational. It was simply the effort it cost him to carry on a conversation. He was at Mike Moorcock's wedding reception, I remember.

D.B: You did quite a few one-off magazines with Mike Moorcock. Could you say anything about them? **ERGO EGO,** for example.

J.C: ERGO EGO was two Aubrey Beardsley fans joining together, Mike Moorcock and myself. That was quite deliberate, of course. A large part of the material was written in that style and therefore had to be illustrated in that style. We did some rather peculiar

Ergo-Ego, 1962 – One of a series of one-off Michael Moorcock fanzines. Cawthorn's artwork deliberately executed in the Beardsley style.

Les Spinge, cover, circa 1963 – A fanzine which contained a number of Moorcock articles illustrated by Cawthorn such as **Spaceship to the Psyche** and **An Angle on Asgard.**

things, particularly **FLAIL,** which carried quite a bit of material by Mike, in particular a film columnist send-up, for which I had to draw caricatures of film stars, which I quite enjoyed. There were a few others, **EUSTACE** and such like. When I first met Mike he was heavily into Rhythm and Blues, work blues and that kind of thing, and I think that I illustrated a couple of pieces in his R & B fanzine.

D.B: You did a number of S & S illustrations in what must have been the least likely journal ever to carry fantasy illustrations, **FLAME,** which was a left-wing political paper.

J.C: Alistair Graham, who was the editor of **TARZAN ADVENTURES** before Mike, became **FLAME's** editor, and naturally Mike contributed. The illustrations must have totally bemused the readership.

D.B: Can you describe the office where **TARZAN ADVENTURES** was produced?

J.C: It was about the size of a large cupboard. It was quite dark because as far as I remember the only window was quite high up on the wall, and very small. It had a table running along the left-hand side as you went in through the door which took up most of that side of the office. Then there was Mike, and a chair, who took up most of the middle of the office, and there was a table at the back which was stacked with thousands of copies of the various publications that IPC did, and that took care of the rest. I remember the whole place, even the Senior Editor, whose office was just through a door in a sub-divided wall; bleak and bare and making no concessions to absolutely anything except Work. My whole impression of that place is that it was bleak and dark and absolutely bare.

D.B: You obviously worked very closely as an illustrator with the magazine **NEW WORLDS** under Moorcock's editorship, both during its early days as a **Compact** paperback and later on the large-format editions. I want to ask you about the illustrations you did for Ballard's **Storm Bird, Storm Dreamer,** for they appear to be drawn in a style that is appreciably starker than any I have seen you use before.

J.C: It is a style that I **have** in fact used before, but you do not see it used commercially. And another thing, it was about the only possible style I could have used given the time I had. The magazine was late to press and five or six of the **NEW WORLDS'** team were sitting around in Mike's study – Diane Lambert, Charles Platt, Mike, myself and possibly Lang Jones. To save time we were proof-reading this particular issue, passing the galleys round hand-to-hand, and I was reading the Ballard story for the first time in proof form, and illustrating it. As I read it, bit by bit, I would illustrate a part of it and then pass that part on to the next person. So that was the only possible style you could do the illustrations in under those circumstances. At the same time, and in the same issue, I had to illustrate an article on Tolkein by Daphne Castell. Incidentally, the **Sunday Telegraph** did an interview with Tolkein for their colour magazine and billed it as the first magazine interview he had given, and of course it wasn't. The **Telegraph** interview came out in print three months after the **NEW WORLDS** interview with him.

D.B: You did a very remarkable series of illustrations for **AMRA** where you experimented with the basic **Sword & Sorcery** figures and drew them in the form of solid black, and sometimes abstract silhouettes. What were you trying to achieve with these?

J.C: I got the idea of trying the visual effect of a solid black figure – which would not really be a silhouette. It was instead posed so as to imply three dimensions. There was a negress in armour with a sword. There was a man in armour with a sword. There was a youth fighting a winged serpent with a knife. I wanted to try the possibilities of using a solid black figure, with the rest of the drawing in outline without any solid black in it, just using black and white for the contrast. The trick was to use the harness and the

Eldritch Dream-Quest, cover, circa 1963 – The first British **Sword & Sorcery** fanzine.

The Jewel in the Skull, cover – White Lion hard cover edition, 1973. First of four **Dorian Hawkmoon** books, each with a Cawthorn cover.

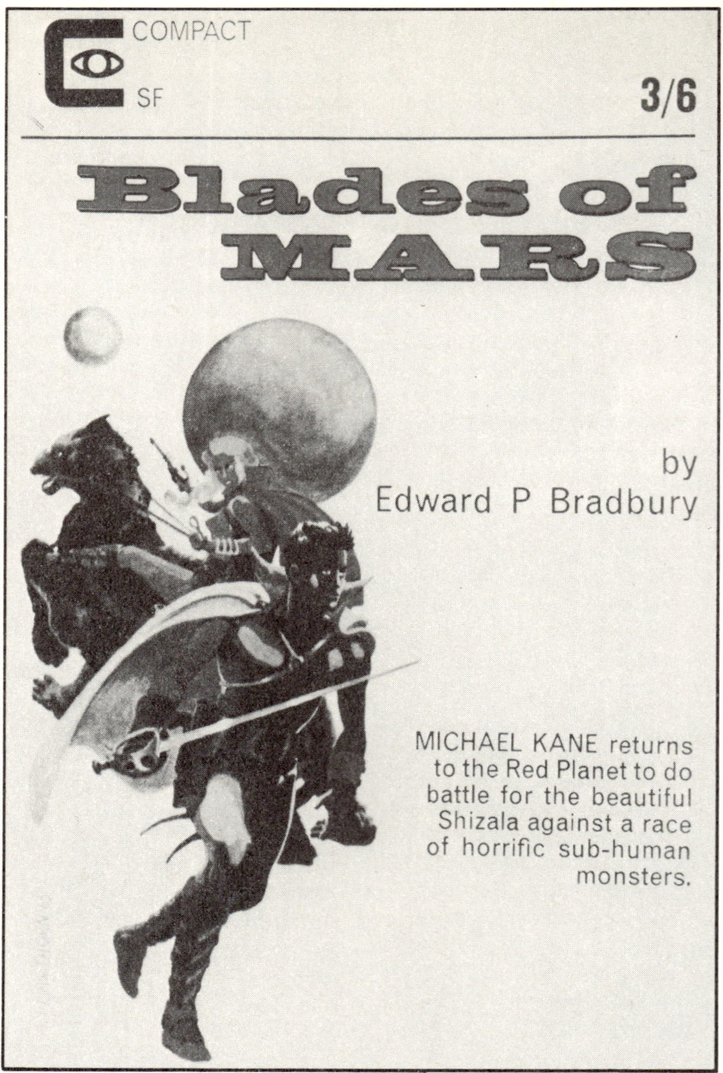

Blades of Mars, cover – A series of three books with Cawthorn covers published by Compact Books, 1965. Edward P. Bradbury was a pseudonym of Michael Moorcock.

clothes that the figures were wearing by suggesting they were curving around the outlines of a three-dimensional figure.

D.B: Your work has developed during various projects over a period of twenty-five years or more, yet you have not been widely recognised except in the last five. The step you've taken from doing single illustrations to the epic strip may have fetched its own problems…

J.C: The fundamental weakness of my artwork is that I do not plan it sufficiently. There are ways of planning the effect that you want to achieve. The only real way to plan a strip is to plan it by the page rather than by the panel – which I do to a certain extent but I ought to be able to do so much more directly to achieve the particular effect I want – whereas I tend to sort of circle around the subject and stab at it. Now and again I hit it, now and again I miss it. This is where people like Hogarth are different. They obviously have to plan out and they obviously know very well in advance what they want in each frame, and they know how they are going to go after it. It's really the only way to approach a strip if you want a consistent level of style. **The Jewel in the Skull** is my longest and best work to date. There are probably as many individual illustrations contained in **Jewel in the Skull,** if you count each panel as an illustration, as there are single illustrations in my entire career to date.

D.B: Jewel is your best. It has, in the words of a recent reviewer, an atmosphere of evil that is 'literally palpable. The hero, Dorian Hawkmoon, sails up the river into the city; bridges, ships, buildings are all alive.' The buildings and atmosphere have a very solid quality.

J.C: It had to be rooted in a quite solid sense of massed stonework, textures, et cetera, because the story itself quite often brings out the texture of things; and those are the best passages in the story, where Mike has time to dwell on the details of things, so that the metal of the armour **feels** like metal, and the stonework **feels** like stone. It's the in between stretches which I think were probably more hastily written, that are the let-downs, the weaker links. I have not come to these yet. The first book, **Jewel,** is quite dense, there are very few gaps of that kind. It's the later books when the heroes begin to travel around.

D.B: There is not much decoration in your work...

J.C: I don't think too much decoration works in **Sword & Sorcery** because it does not produce **action,** and the genre needs to have movement: a page of **Jewel** for instance is more like the pace of Foster's **Prince Valiant** than say a Caniff or a Hogarth! Decoration, certainly, in order to given an impression of the richness of the background, the trappings and the dress, but that has to be incidental to the action, because, above everything else it has to **move.** Decoration works in the decorative arts, for the Pre-Raphaelites and such people. The whole recent fantasy scene has been trying to reproduce a feeling of hallucination and drug-effects in artistic terms...

D.B: But there is more than a little of this mood and feel running throughout **Jewel.** The LSD scene, in particular the hallucinogenic gases.

J.C: Yes, they actually are bubbles of hallucinogenic gases, but that particular episode specified that these people were being affected by hallucinogenic gases. That particular scene could not be decorative in any way – it had to be terrifying. It had to say something which would terrify a group of people who were themselves well into hallucination. Its basis is actually more in religious imagery.

D.B: In certain areas the Hawkmoon stories offer more scope for an artist than, say, the Elric sagas.

J.C: Yes, because they are more firmly tied to a realistic background and they offer a mixture of what is actually Science Fiction and pure Fantasy. The Science Fiction is of a kind that I particularly like, which is a form of Victorian futurism. In other words it's super science based upon an essentially mediaeval society, which ties in a lot of scenes I saw when I was a kid and I was brought up amongst the remains of Nineteenth Century industrialism which are quite fantastic; the shapes of the ironwork and the machinery, with which I was surrounded as a child.

D.B: You are probably best known for your illustrations for Michael Moorcock's books – **Stormbringer, Sojan, Behold the Man, The Golden Barge, Warlord of the Air,** et cetera. Are there any books you missed illustrating?

J.C: I missed doing an edition of **Stealer of Souls** for which I still have the preliminary illustrations. I did a page of Elric strip early on that has not been seen. For **FRENDZ** magazine I did a large Elric poster that was scheduled to be printed over the centre pages, but the magazine folded before it could be used.

D.B: How did the first Elric drawing come about?

J.C: Part of **The Flame Bringers** was originally written as a non-Elric story, and I drew an illustration of the central character. Mike then changed this to Elric by rubbing out the pupils of the eyes, so that they were blank like the Elves' eyes in Anderson's **The Broken Sword,** which is what he was probably thinking of at the time, and that was one of the first drawings of Elric. Later, Mike incorporated this story into **The Flame Bringers.**

D.B: Wasn't there a similar origin to the Elric story **Kings in Darkness?**

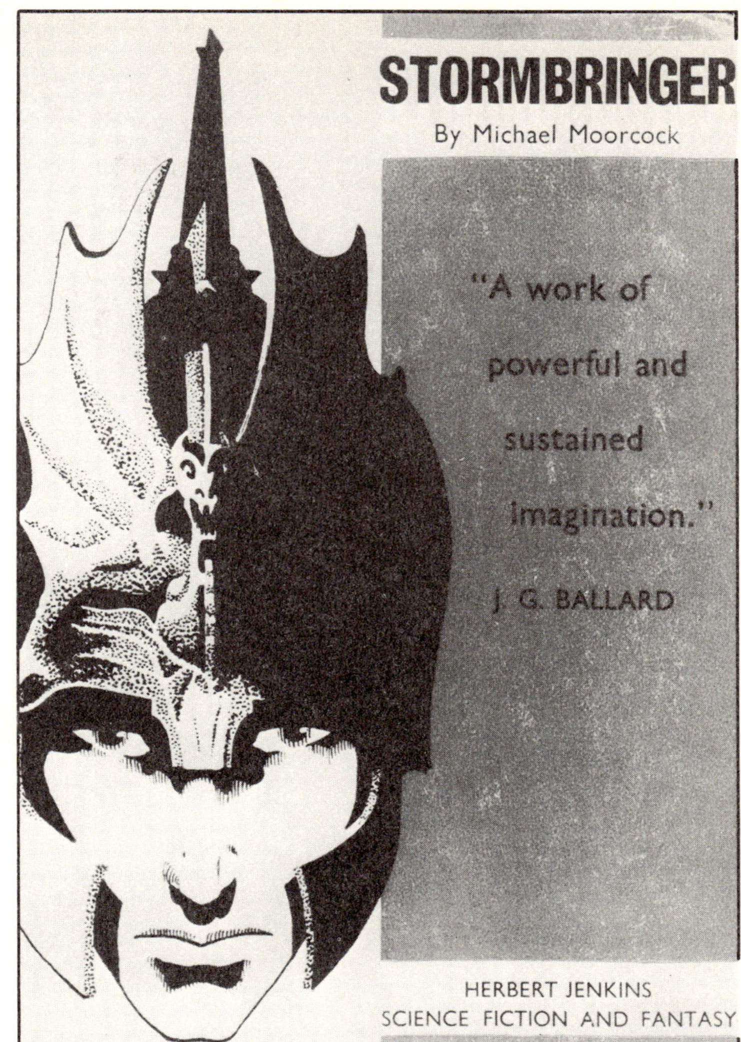

Stormbringer, cover – First hard cover edition, 1965, published by Herbert Jenkins.

Science Fantasy No.55, 1962 – First publication of Elric story, **The Flame Bringers.**

J.C: I wrote the plot of it, certainly. And one or two of the bits of description that I used appeared in the story. The reason it never really worked as an Elric story is that it was meant originally to be a Conan story. The girl Zarozinia was added by Mike of course. Since the story, as it stood, would have been too short and too weak. It was intended as a very short Conan adventure, just a typical straight-forward kind of thing. Possibly because I know its origin I have never really felt that it works, and I know that Mike doesn't either.

D.B: Coming back to your style, which has changed considerably over the years. Who are your influences?

J.C: My early commercial drawings were influenced by Rubens and Michaelangelo. The two different styles – the earlier, cleaner, more formally posed work, and the later, rougher, sketchier style, are now integrated into one. There are also very few differences between the drawings I do for myself and the commercial artwork. In the very beginning the commercial artwork looked a lot stiffer and less natural, less spontaneous. The first time Mike got a commercial drawing from me it could have been from some other artist as far as he was concerned. I think he was rather disappointed. He would see the rather dynamic preliminary sketches, which he really liked, and the finished artwork would be a very formal thing, similar to the early Sojan drawings. I used waverly nibs a great deal at this particular time, which contributed to the appearance. Going back to influences, with regard to the stiple effects I use, the Impressionists were a key influence. That early style was based on the monumental figures that many classical artists used. The massive, heroically-proportioned figures were very similar to the figures of S & S heroes. But my subject matter was fantasy of the **Planet Stories** kind. I also used this style a great deal for Science Fiction type of illustrations.

D.B: I remember seeing an American magazine cover that you had rendered very much in the Mervyn Peake manner, but you had used your stencil technique.

J.C: How Many Miles to Babylon. There was also another illustration I did in the same mould, of children riding on a griffin. It

Page from Cawthorn's unpublished strip adaptation of Robert E. Howard's **Shadows in Zamboula,** 1957, when the artist was 25.

Bognor Regis (Ed David Britton), interior, 1972 – One of six stencils taken from a portfolio by Cawthorn of **The Two Towers** (the second book of Professor Tolkein's **Lord of the Rings** trilogy).

was a direct copy of Peake's black and white illustration. At the same time I put onto stencil two very simple line drawings from **The Quest for Sita,** which was another book Peake illustrated.

D.B: Your most successful stencil illustrations were for Tolkein's **Lord of the Rings.** Have you any future plans for using this technique.

J.C: I did in fact do some stencil work last year, but only in a non-commercial capacity. It is possible that I will do more, perhaps for the four Henry Treece novels you and **Savoy** are publishing in 1979. I will see how the initial stencils for **The Great Captains** materialise before I commit myself!

D.B: For the future, are there any long-term projects that you would particularly like to embark on?

J.C: It has been a long-term, cherished idea of mine to do an illustrated version of **A Princess of Mars.** But I suspect that there will be a difficulty obtaining permission from the Edgar Rice Burroughs Corporation. I have yet to see a version that in any way captures the full Burroughs flavour. If the opportunity arises I would be particularly pleased.

D.B: Finally, to current work. Apart from the Treece books, you are presently illustrating a very interesting book by Mike Moorcock, which is to be published in 1979 by **Pierrot** and distributed by **Big O.**

J.C: This is a book about the history of Fantasy as a genre and presents a very special problem from the artist's point of view. I have to condense the essence of a number of classic fantasy books by authors like Leigh Bracket, Jack Vance, C.L. Moore, et cetera, into single spot illustrations that will be instantly recognisable to the aware reader. To capture something of the atmosphere and subject-matter of so varied a selection is a job I find very difficult indeed, but it is one I am enjoying immensely.

For further interviews readers are referred to **Vortex** Vol. I, No. 1, 1977 and **Science Fiction Monthly** Vol. I, No. 12, 1974.